THE SEARCH FOR KONG

HarperCollins®, ☷®, and HarperKidsEntertainment™ are trademarks of HarperCollins Publishers.
King Kong: The Search for Kong
Printed in the United States of America.
No part of this book may be used or reproduced in any manner whatsoever without written permission except in the case of brief quotations embodied in critical articles and reviews.
For information address HarperCollins Children's Books, a division of HarperCollins Publishers, 1350 Avenue of the Americas, New York, NY 10019.
www.harperchildrens.com
www.kingkongmovie.com
Library of Congress catalog card number: 2005928978
ISBN-10: 0-06-077303-0 — ISBN-13: 978-0-06-077303-8
❖

KONG

THE 8TH WONDER OF THE WORLD™

THE SEARCH FOR KONG

Adapted by Catherine Hapka

Illustrated by Peter Bollinger and Robert Papp

Based on a Motion Picture Screenplay by Fran Walsh &
Philippa Boyens & Peter Jackson

Based on a Story by Merian C. Cooper and Edgar Wallace

HarperKidsEntertainment

An Imprint of HarperCollinsPublishers

ROARRRR! King Kong has scooped up Ann! Her friends chase the two of them across Skull Island.

The men tiptoe through the jungle. *CRACK!*
What was that noise?

Bang! Bang!
They shoot their guns in all directions.
Zzzt. Someone lights a flare.

The men see what they just shot: dinosaurs!
"Aren't those supposed to be extinct?" one of them asks. This island
seems very strange so far. . . .

The men rest in a valley. A herd of brontosauruses graze nearby. Suddenly . . .

STAMPEDE! Carnotaurs race into the valley and chase the peaceful brontosauruses!

Huge, leathery feet crash down all around.
Run!

The men sprint for their lives. The carnotaurs chase them up a steep, mossy slope.

After escaping the carnotaurs, the group reaches a misty, foul-smelling swamp. "We have to get across this!" their leader commands. They build a raft and start across the rotting swamp.

SPLASH!
A repulsive, slimy beast rises out of the water!

RAAAAARRRRR! The swamp creature attacks. The men cling to the raft for their lives.

The group escapes the swamp creature.
But they aren't out of danger. . . .

ROARRRR!!!
It's Kong! He gnashes his crooked, broken teeth and shakes the log the men are crossing.

Kong tips the log and the men fall into a chasm one by one. Thick vines break their fall.

GLUP! GLUP! Huge, ugly maggots suddenly attack, covering everything with slime.

Giant crablike spiders join in: *CLICK, CLICK, CLICK!* Their pincers snap viciously at the men. The men punch and shoot the spiders. Finally they beat back the horrible creatures and escape.

The men have survived all the island's hideous beasts so far.
But will they ever find Ann . . . and Kong?